To the dreamers and believers that keep the story going.... Thank you

Copyright © 2015 All Rights Reserved, Travis Hanson & Bean Leaf Press. Unauthorized reproduction except for the purpose of review is prohibited by law. Title logo, Bean Leaf Press Logo and all characters and art are copyright © 2002 by Travis Hanson. The chapters in this book were originally published in the comic book The Bean and are copyright © 2002 by Travis Hanson.

For contact information, subscription or letters to the artist, please send all inquiries to
Bean Leaf Press
P.O. Box 6495
Moreno Valley CA 92554

Softcover ISBN 978-1-4507-9719-1
Printed in USA
Special thanks to Cathy Hanson, Victoria Morris, Joshua Villines, and Janell for the book edits.

the BEAN
the Dark Road

by Travis Hanson

the Codger

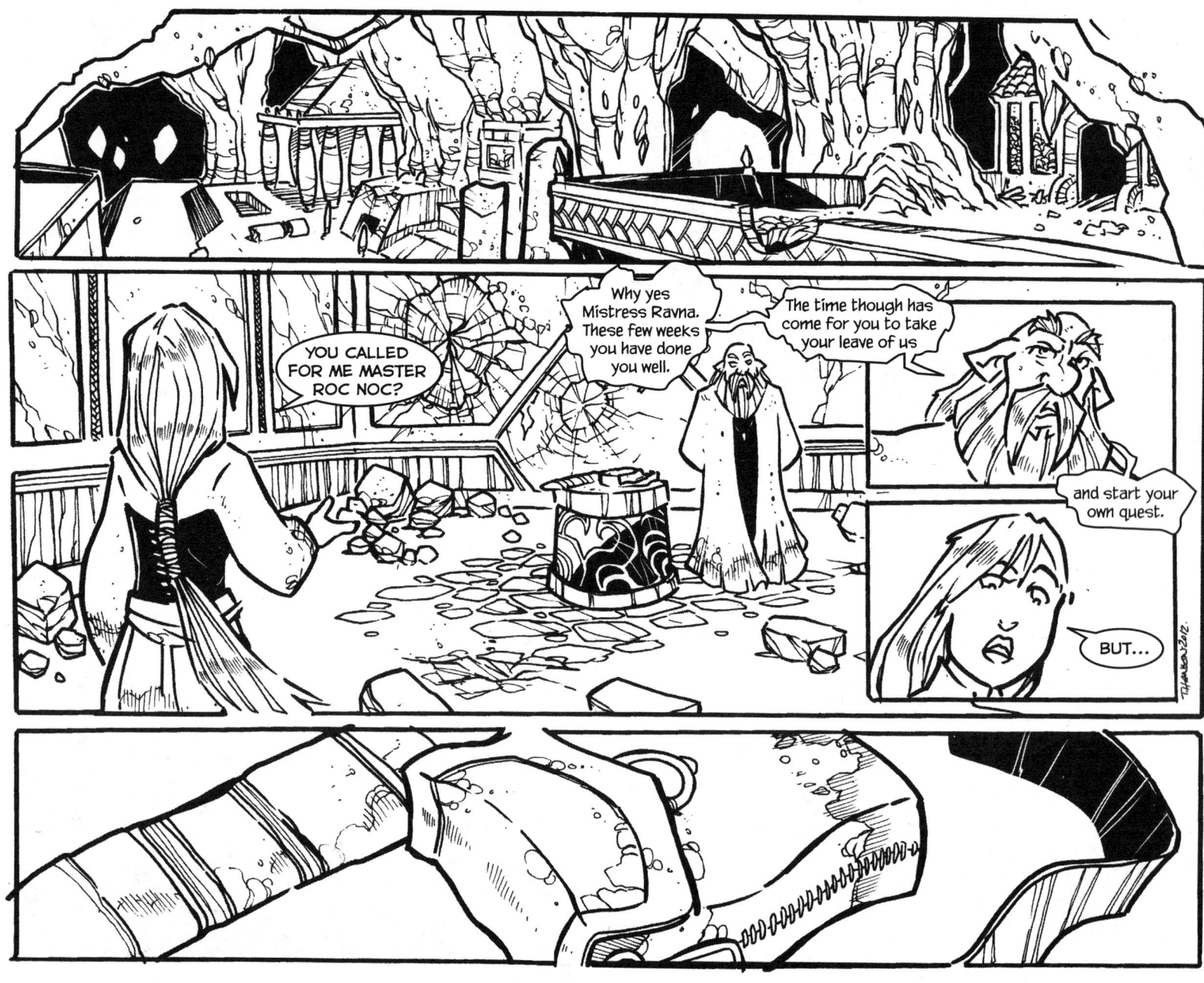

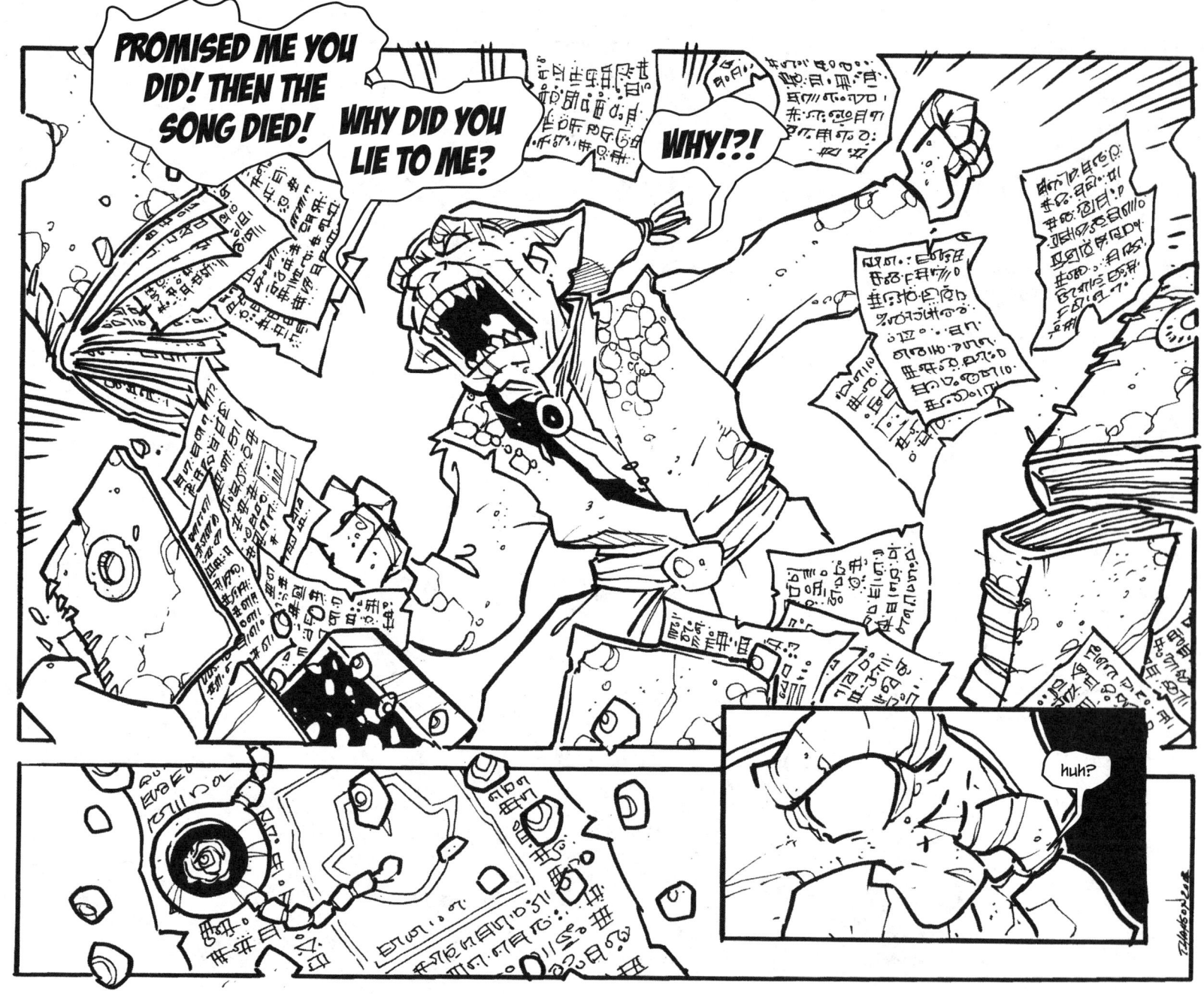

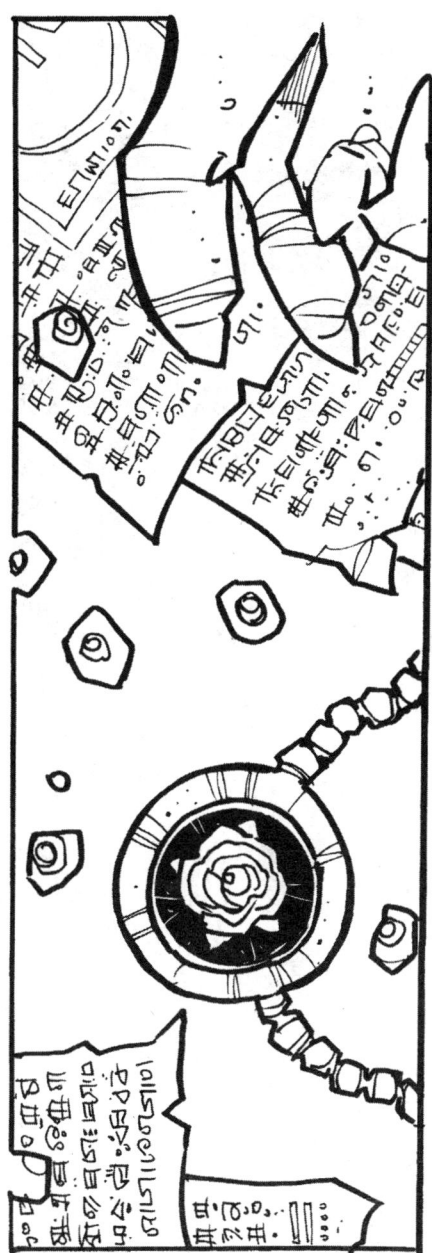

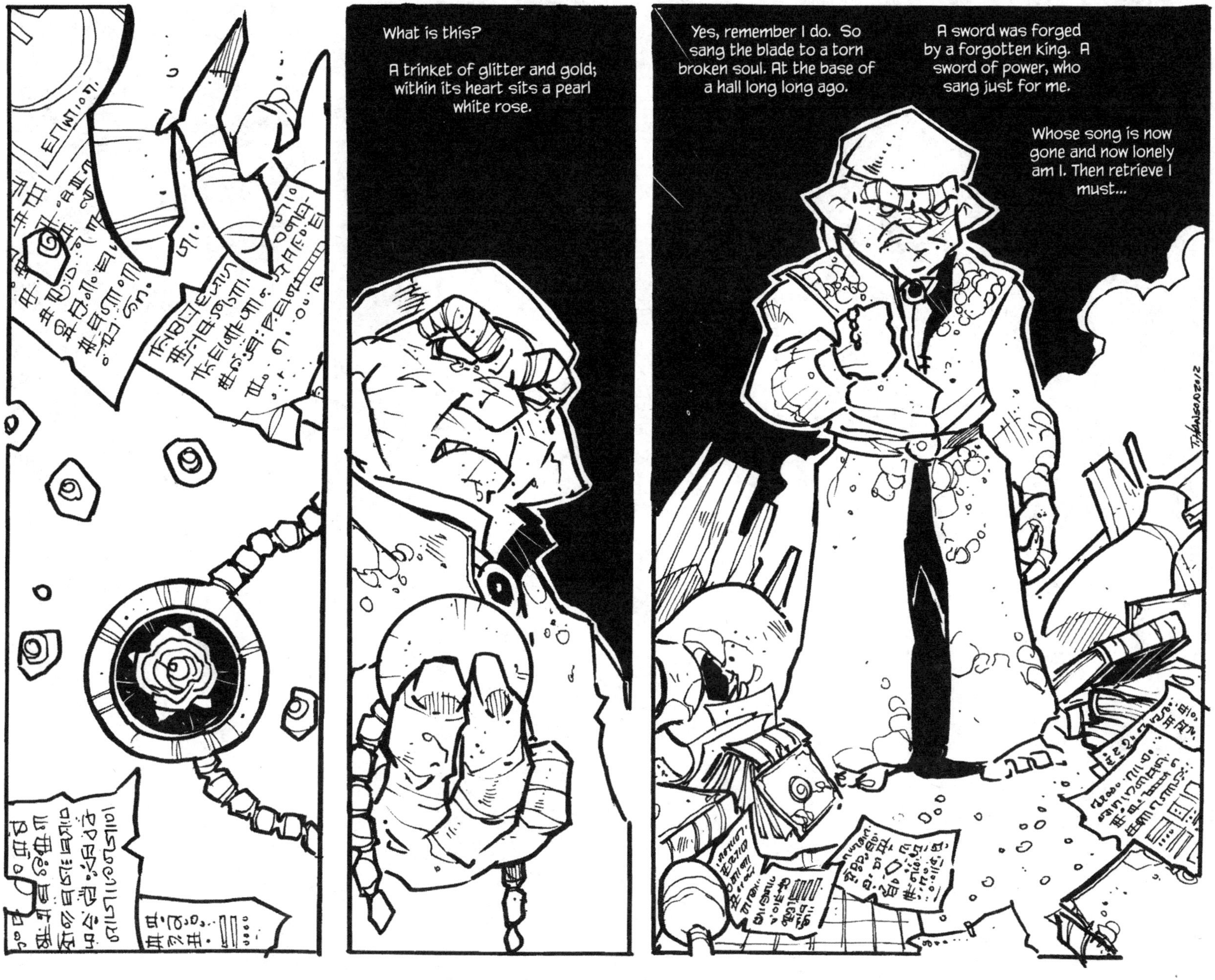

What is this?

A trinket of glitter and gold; within its heart sits a pearl white rose.

Yes, remember I do. So sang the blade to a torn broken soul. At the base of a hall long long ago.

A sword was forged by a forgotten king. A sword of power, who sang just for me.

Whose song is now gone and now lonely am I. Then retrieve I must...

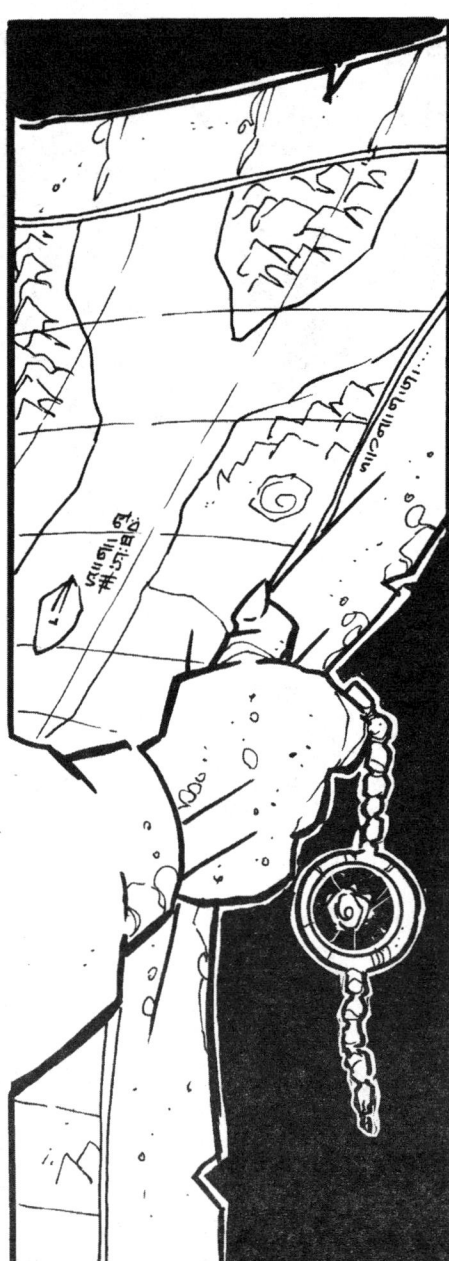

Forgotten had I that sword was forged there. Yet clear is its purpose, the more I dwell here.

For the dead elf's claim still rests in the blade, wielded in the hands of a gopher, a knave.

It matters not. Just a mere hiccup. For now I know where my journey goes and what must I do to find my rose.

To the White Hall I go. To hunt and to see. To find my prize now stolen from me.

For there must he go, the gopher the lad to aid the king when all is bad.

But in for a shock, my gopher will be, for I, the collector, will be waiting you see.

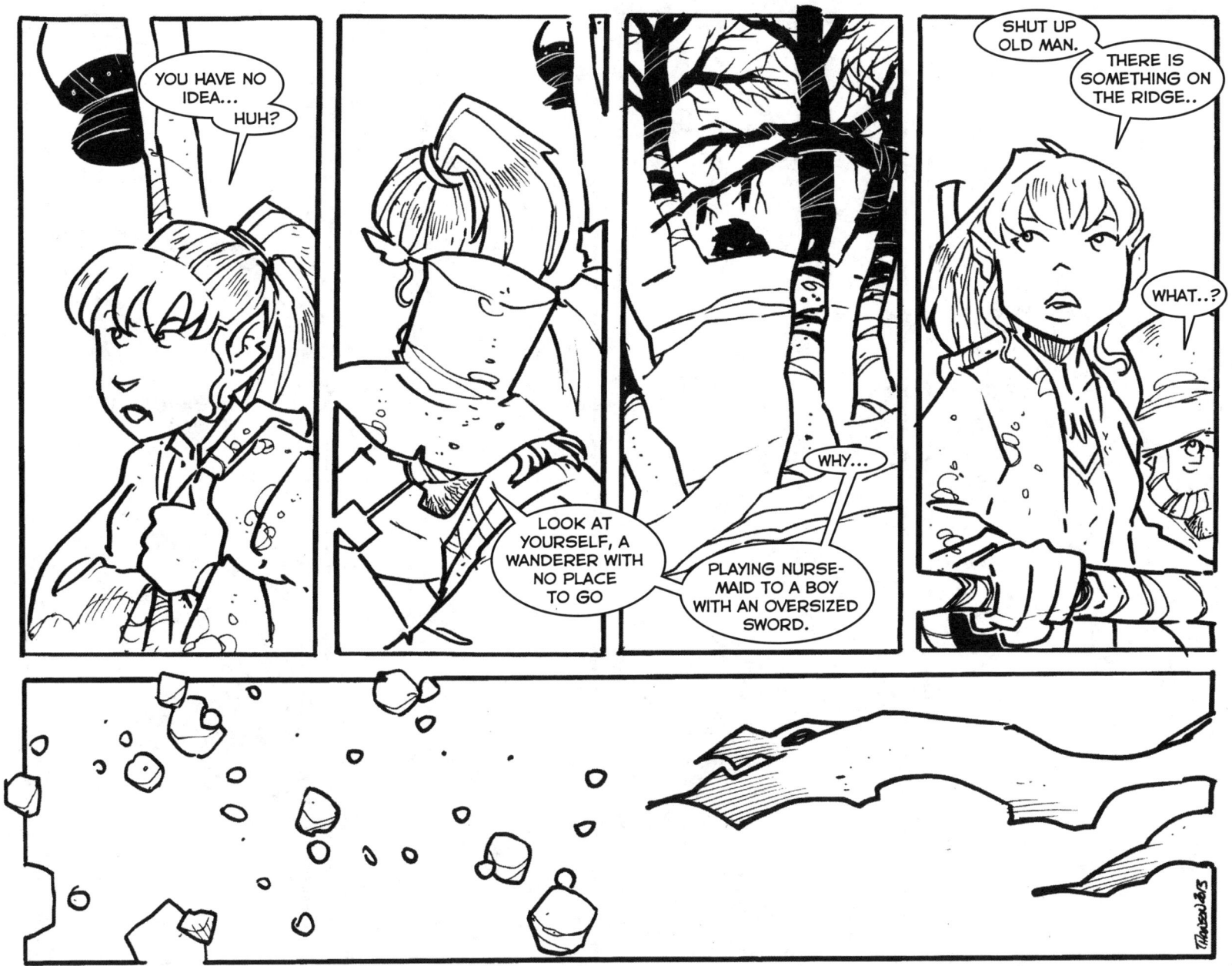

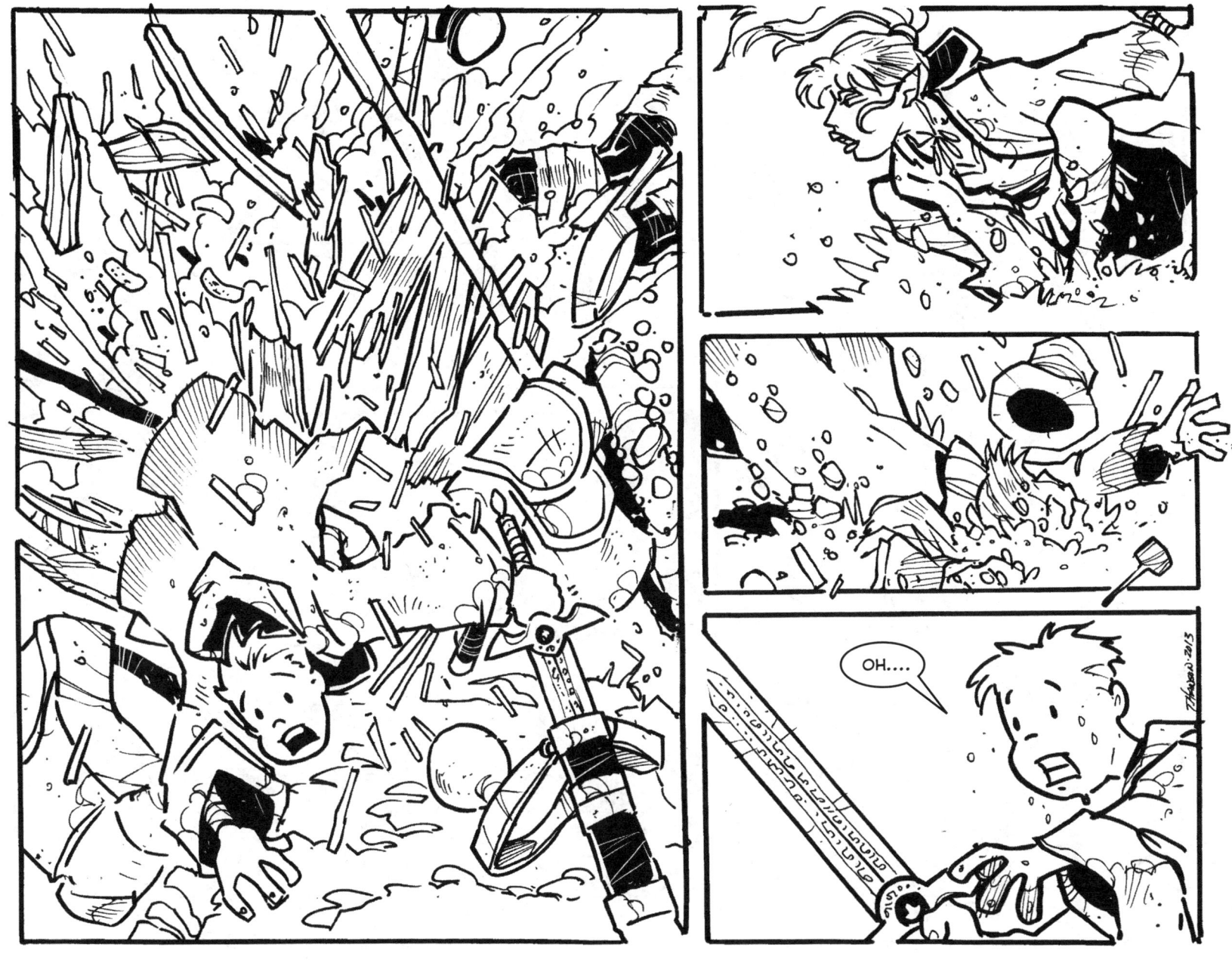

Wandering Souls

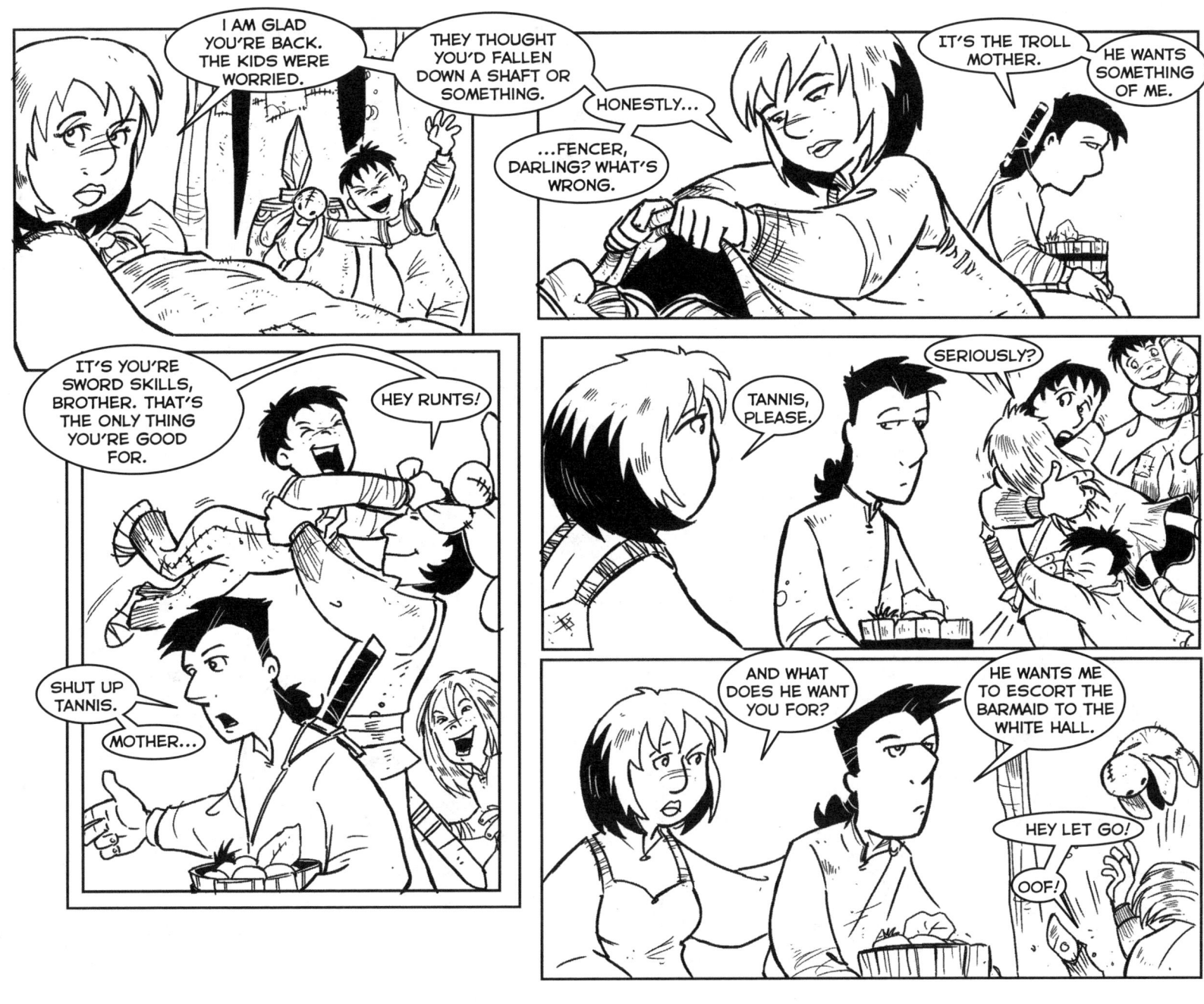

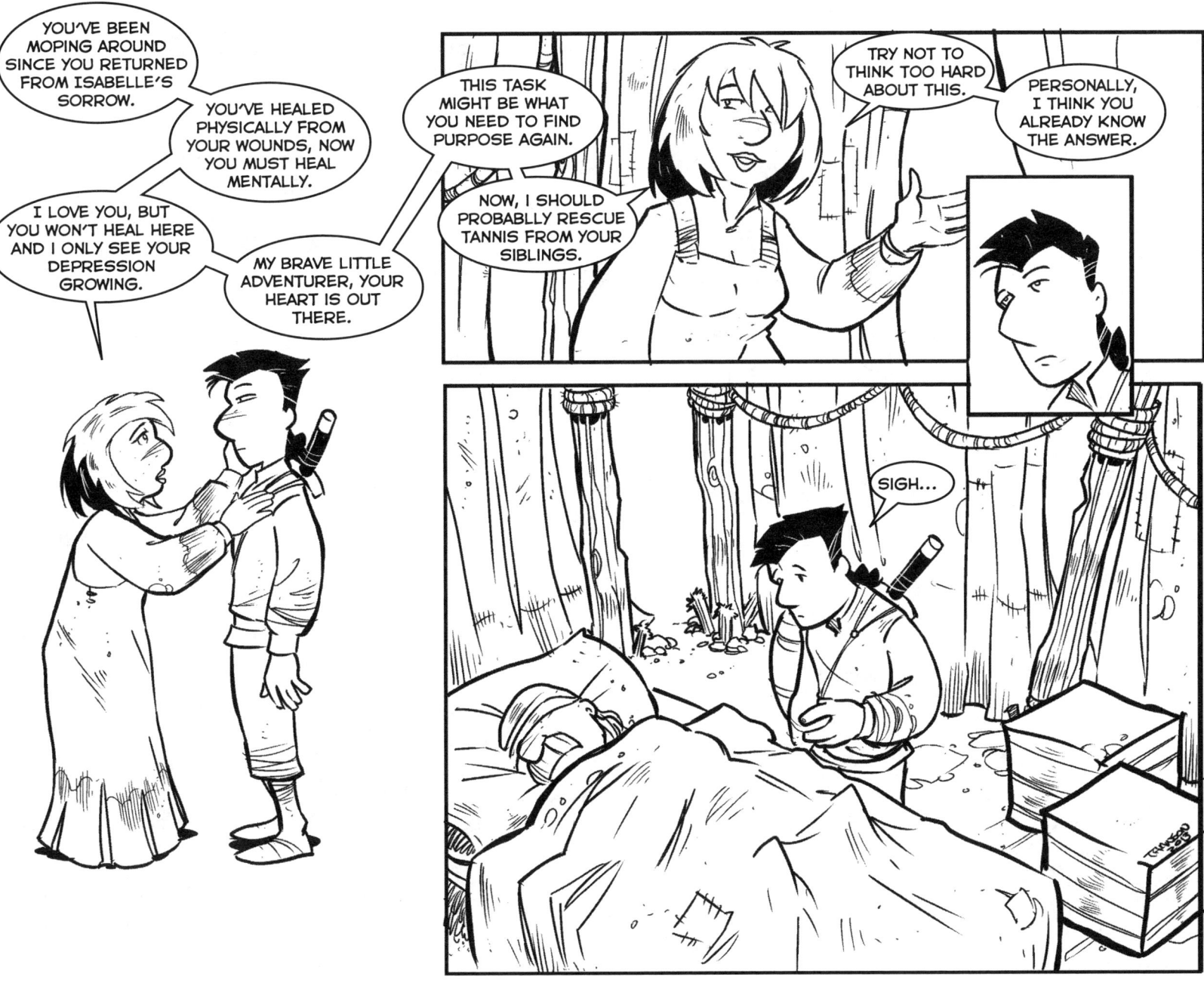

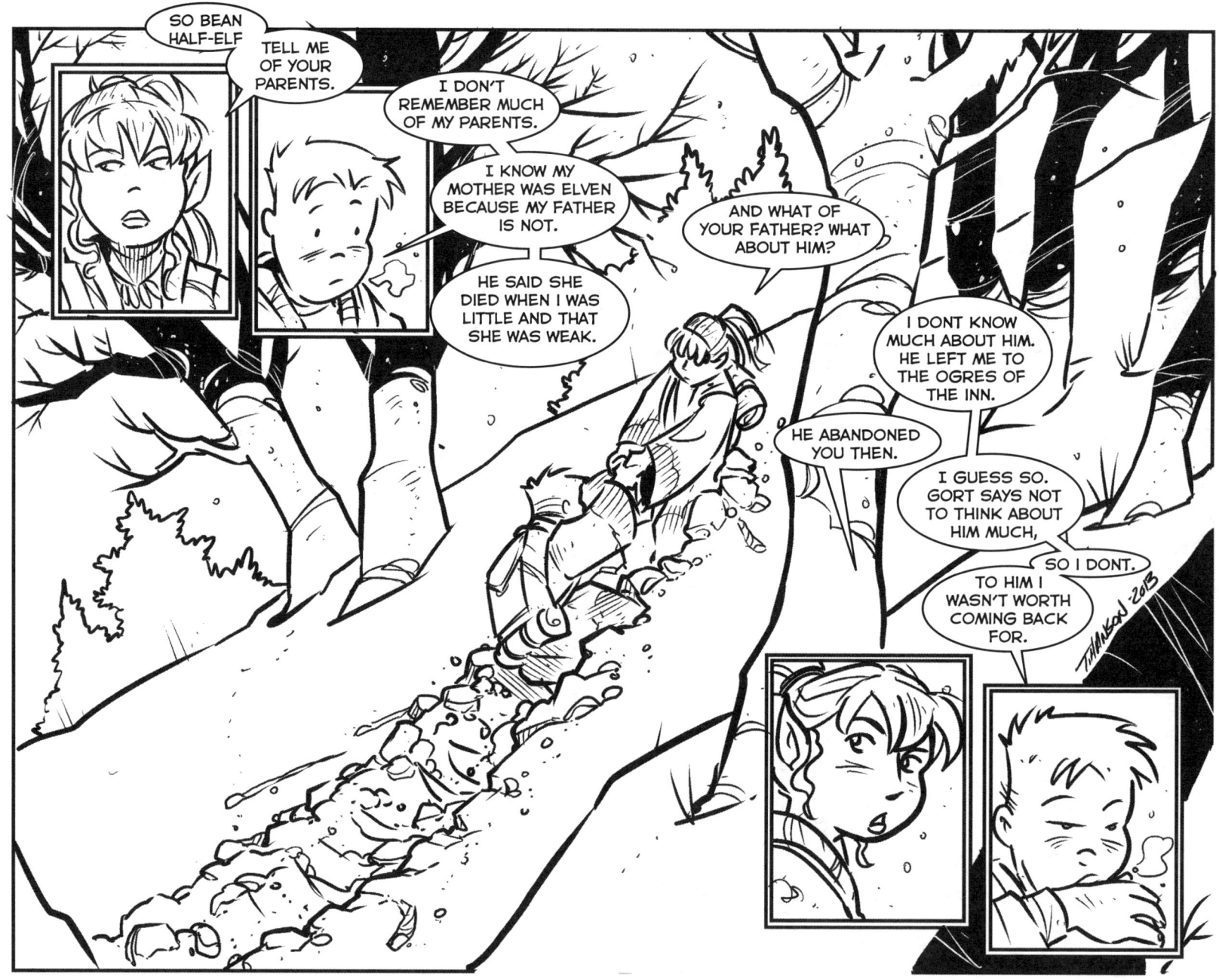

A Warm Heart

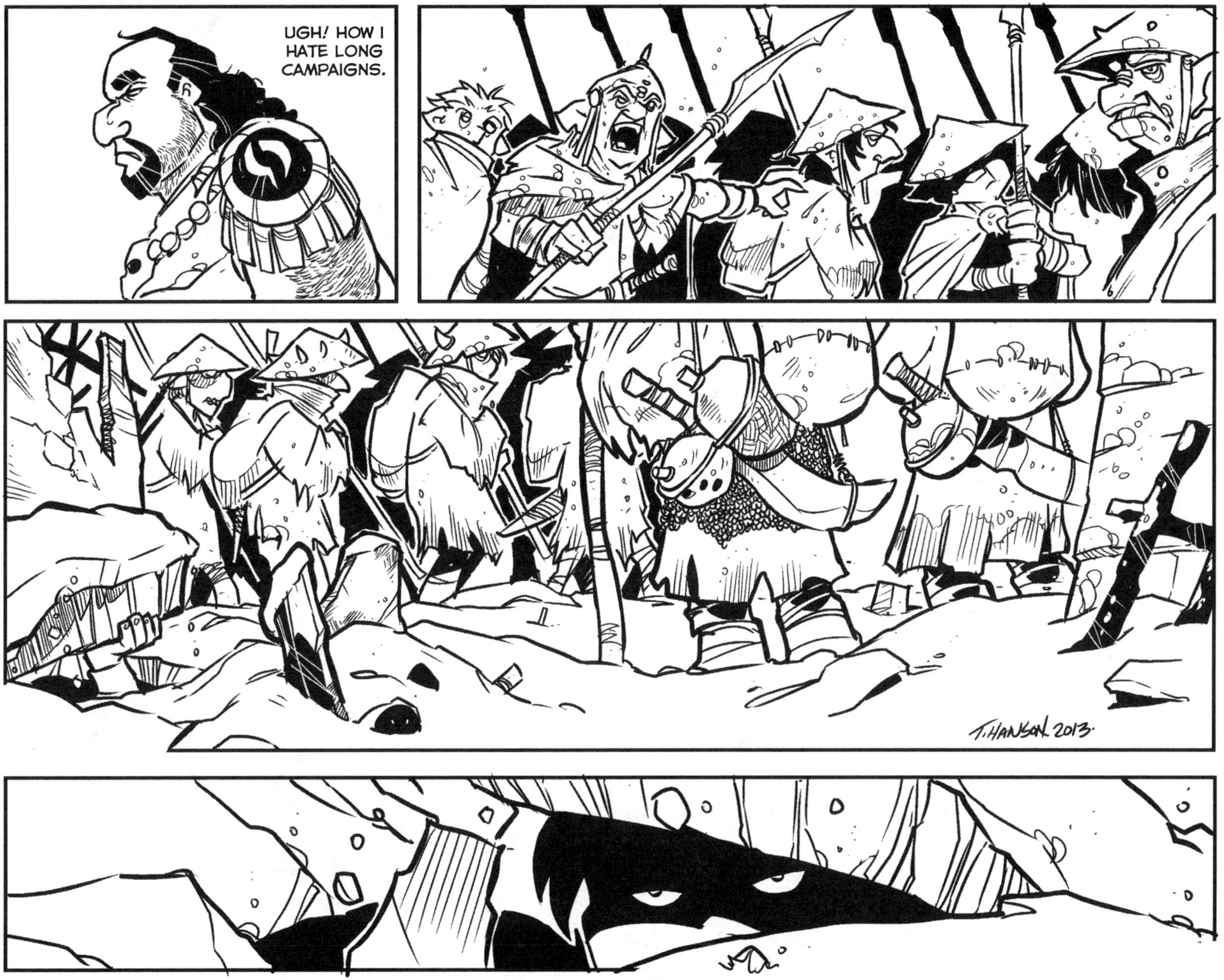

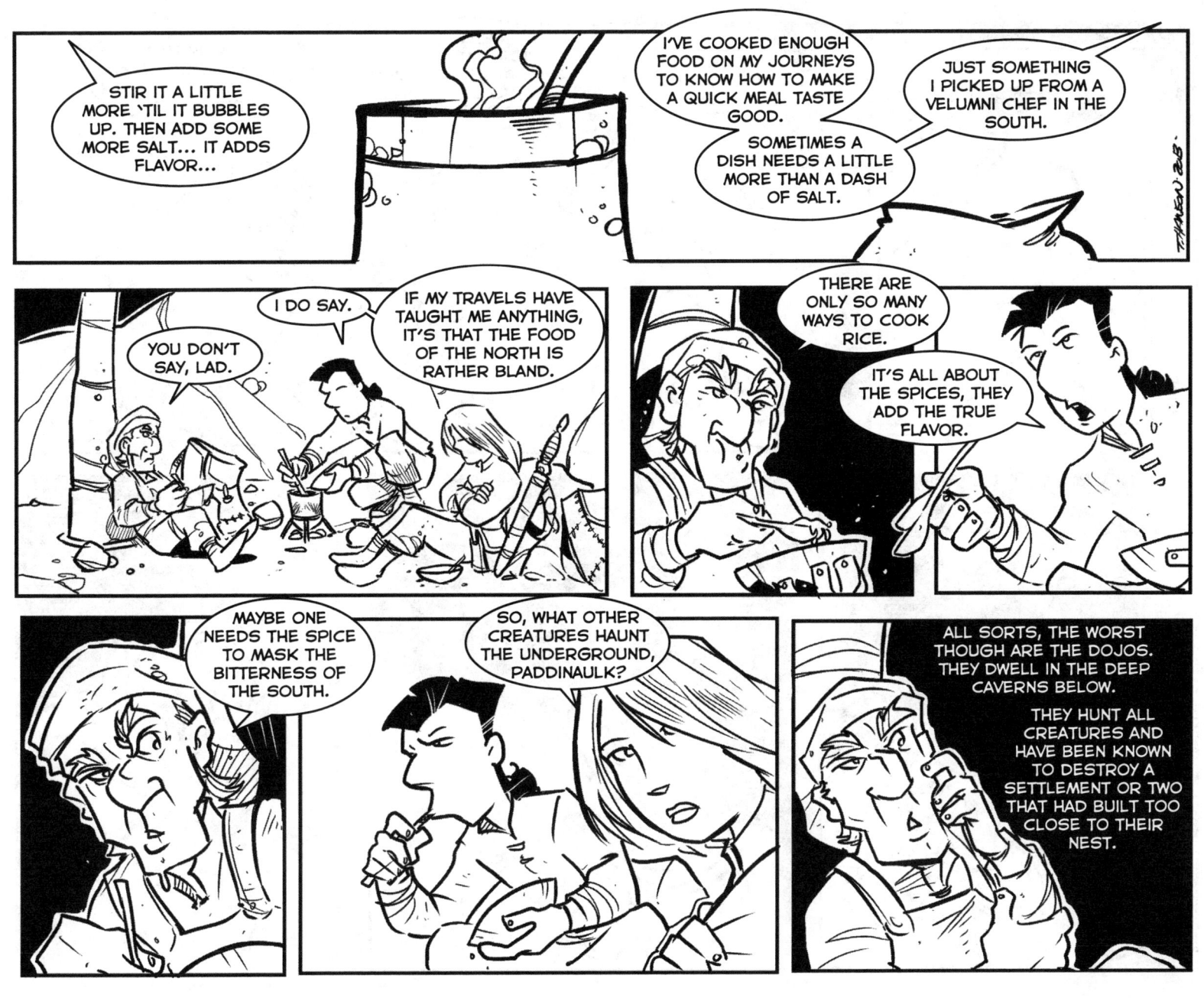

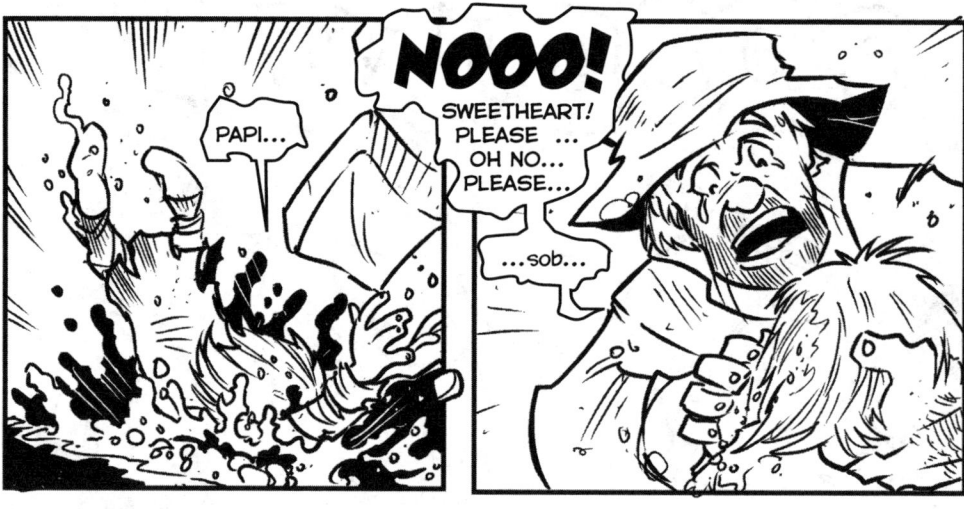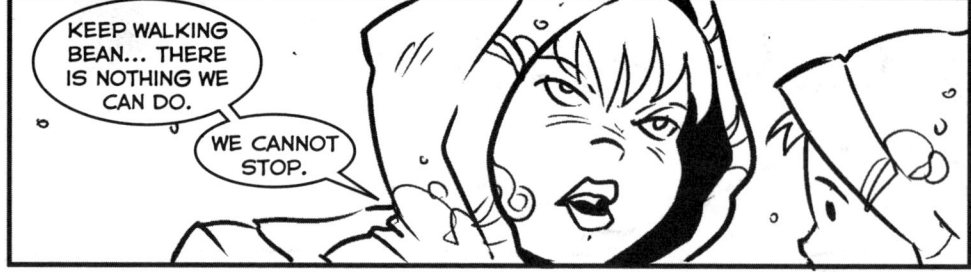

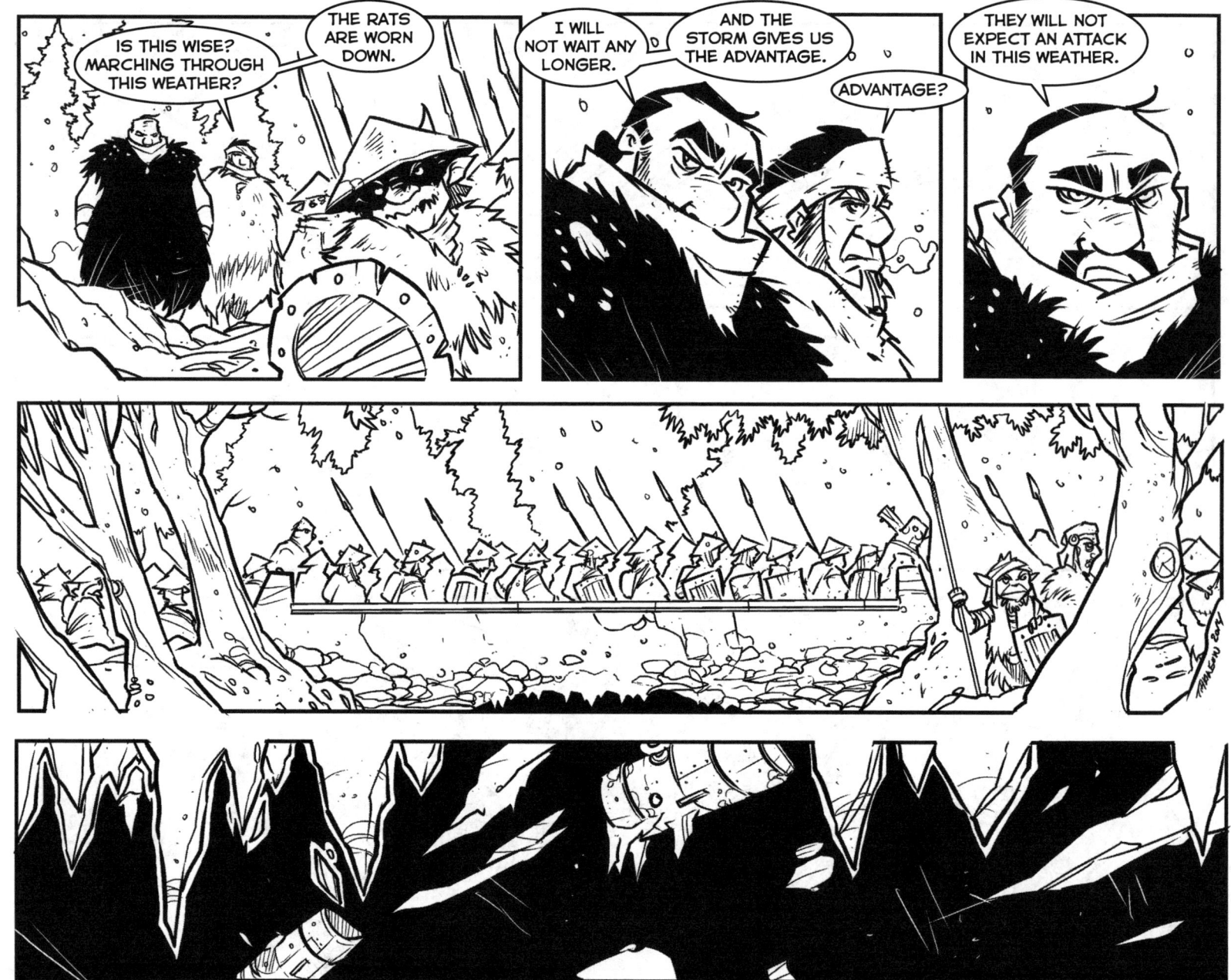

"CLICK"

Culver's Gulch

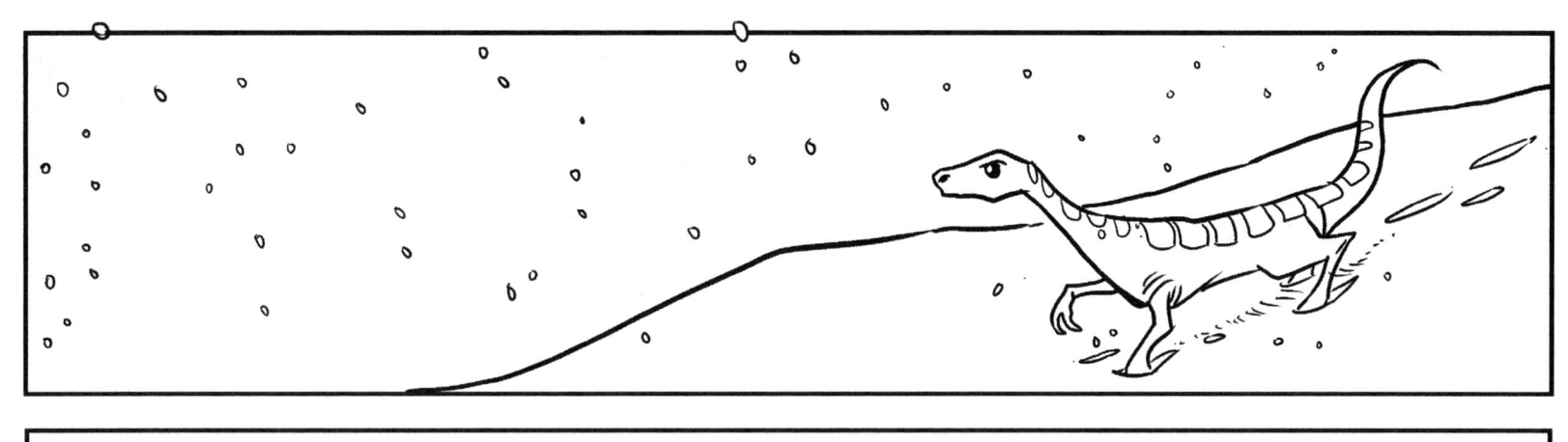

I'VE NEVER BEEN IN A CITY THIS BIG BEFORE.

THIS ISN'T A CITY BEAN.

IT'S A PIT.

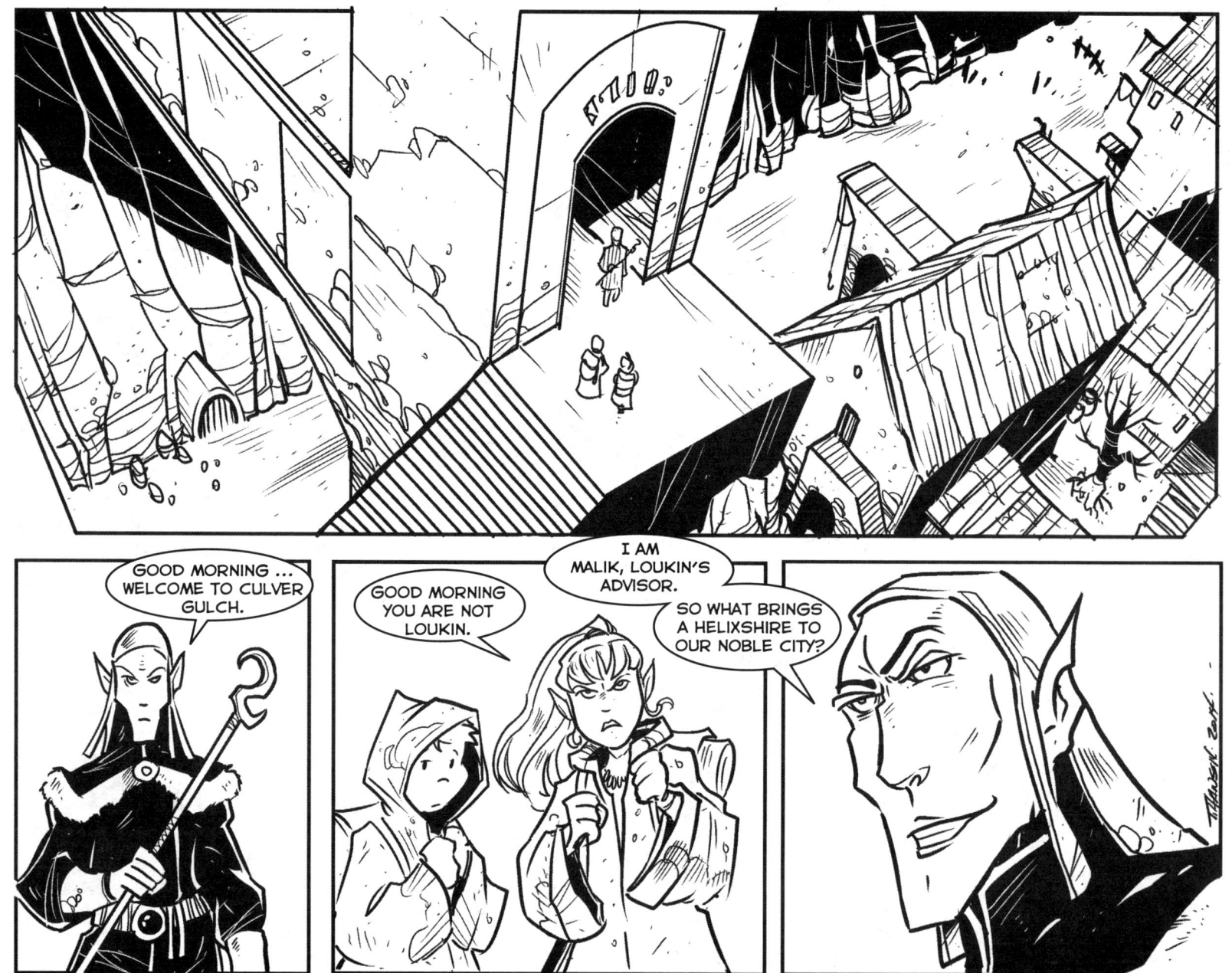

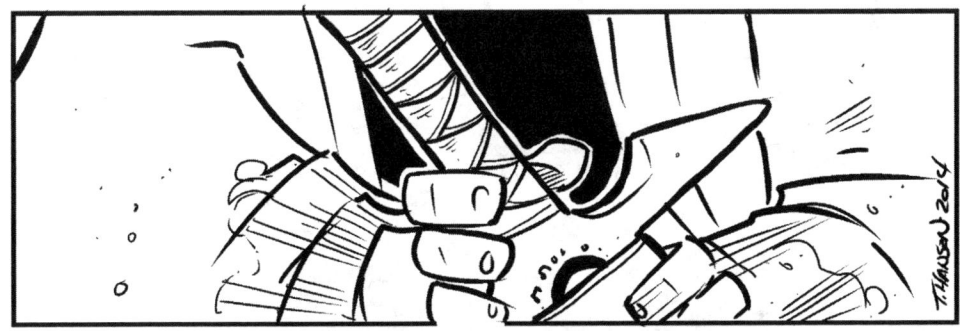

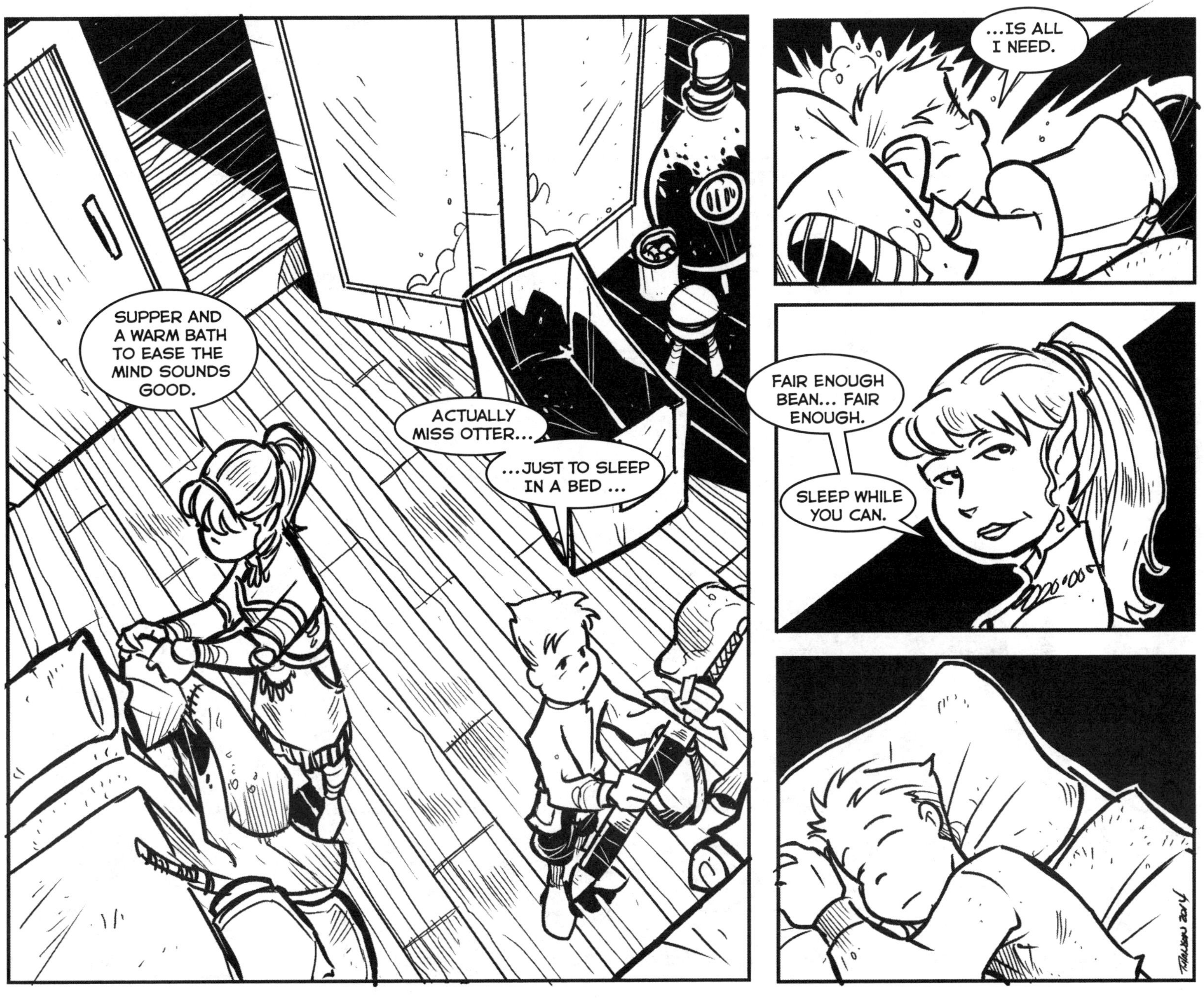

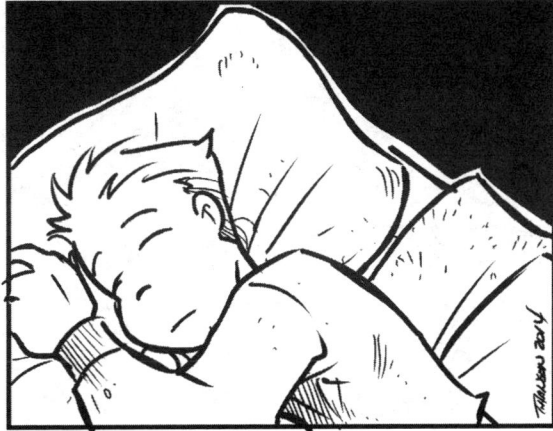

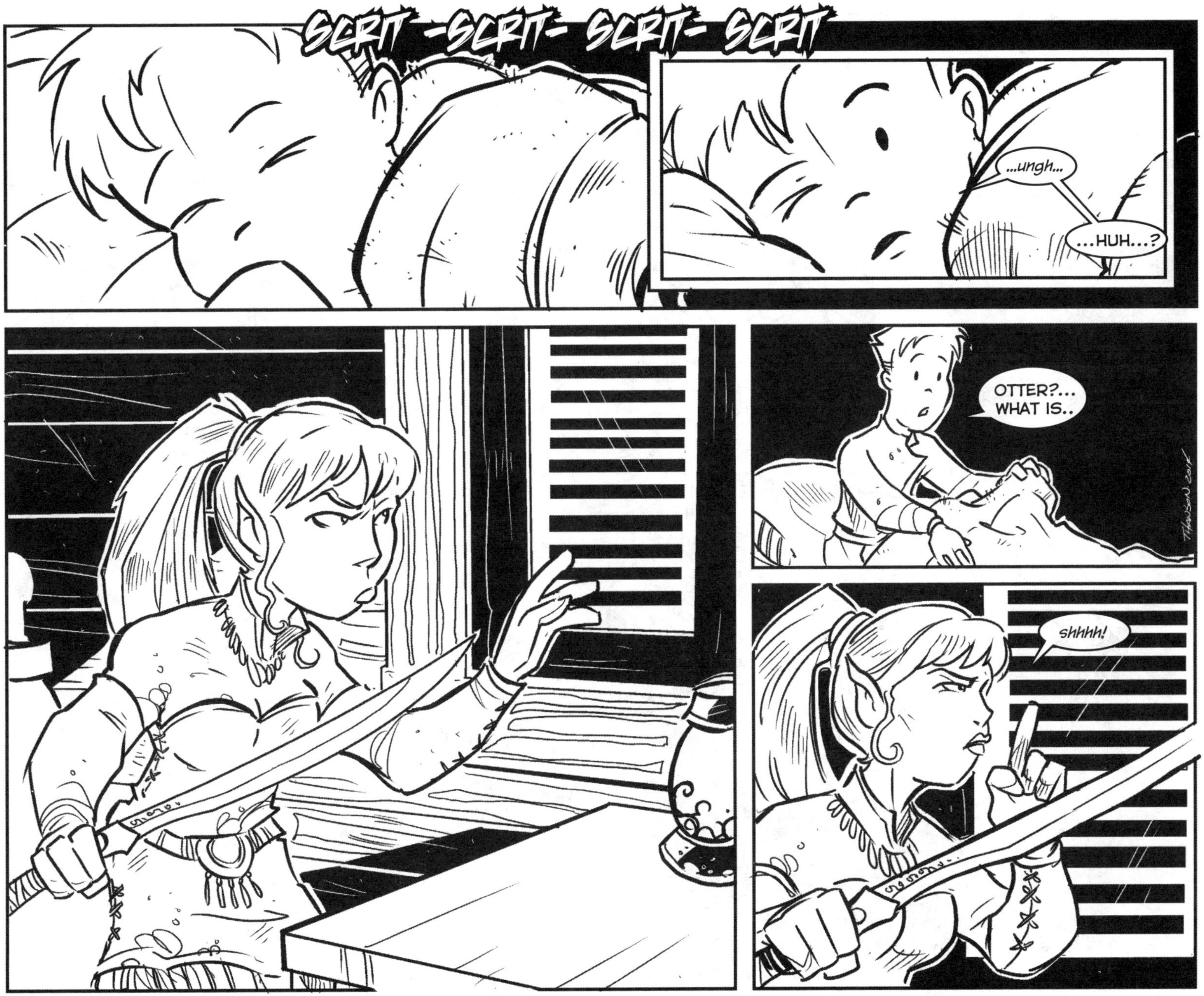

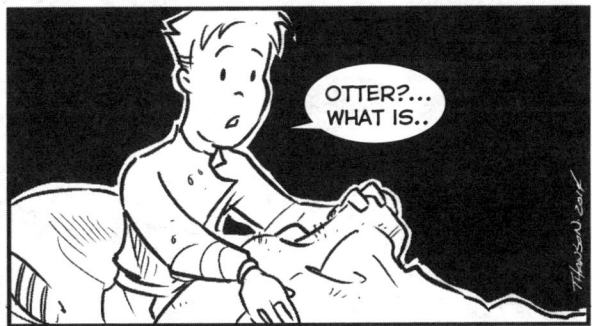

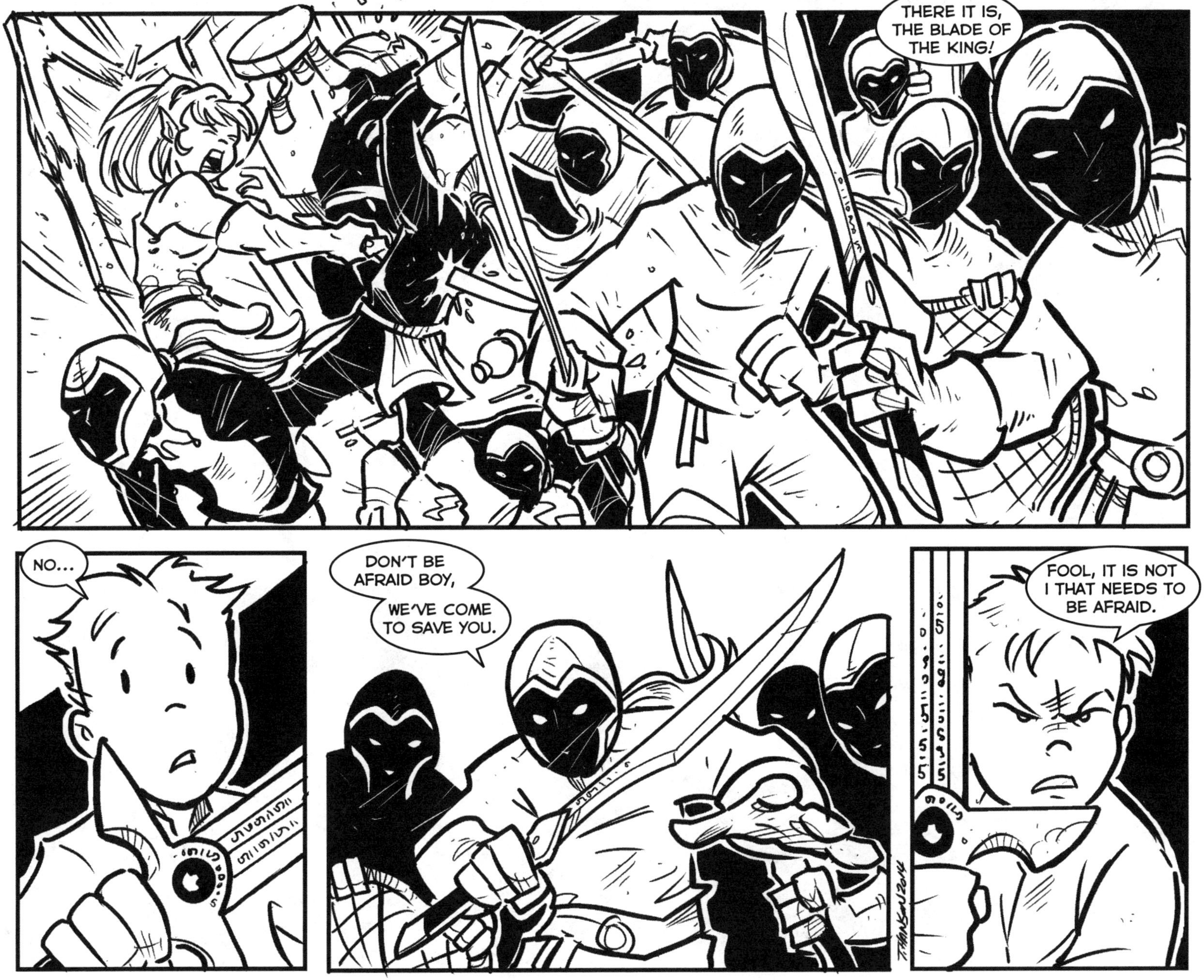

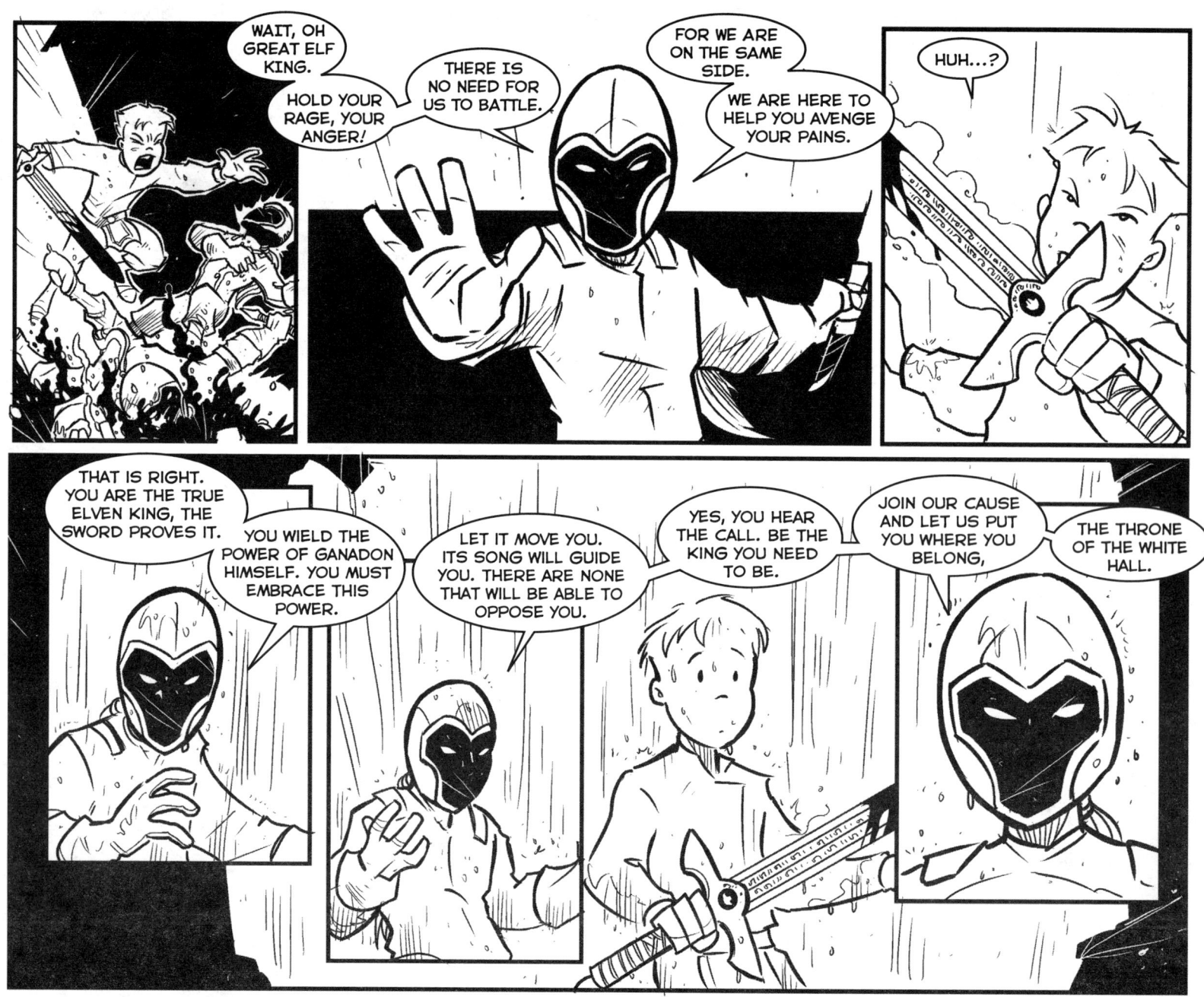

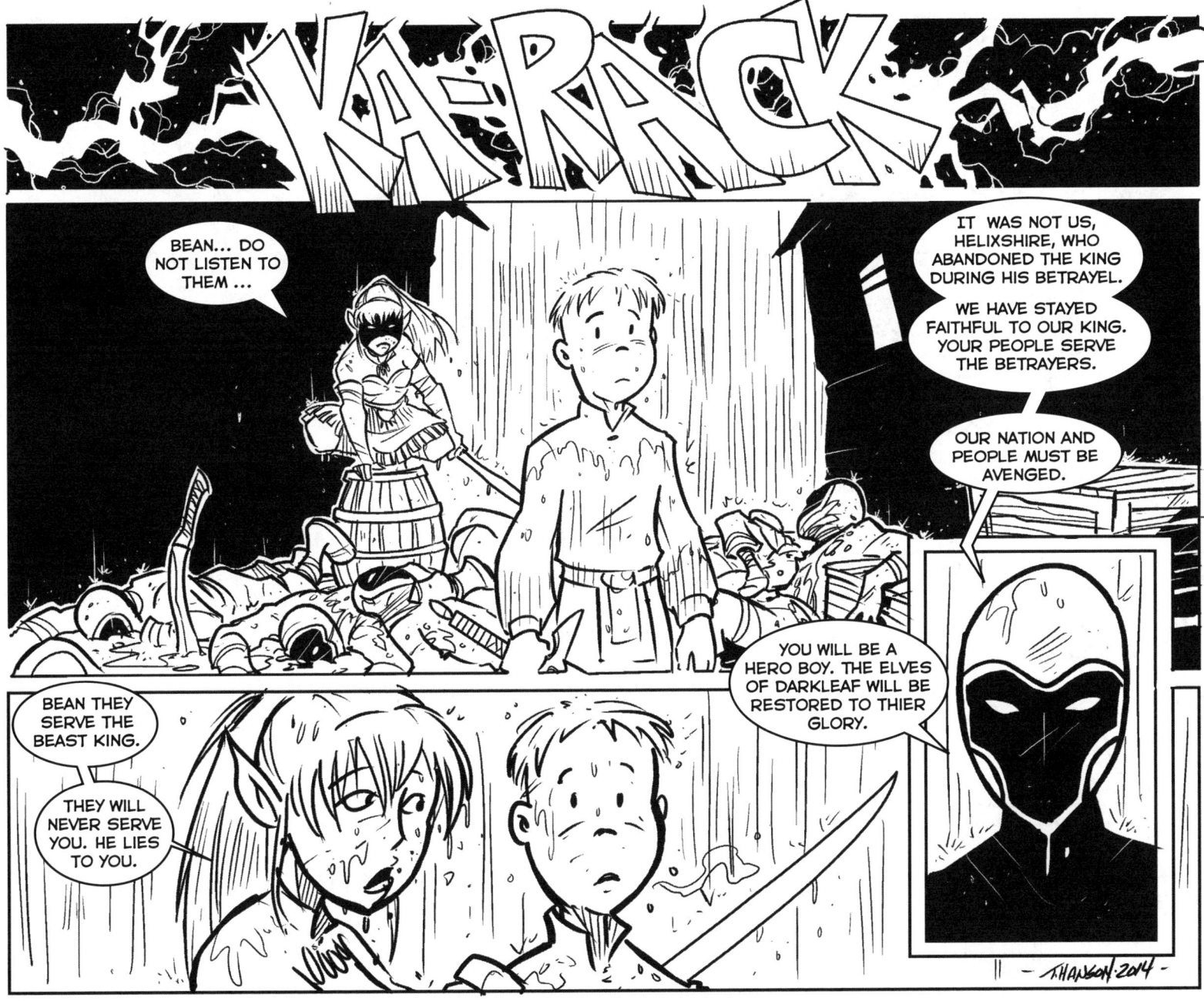

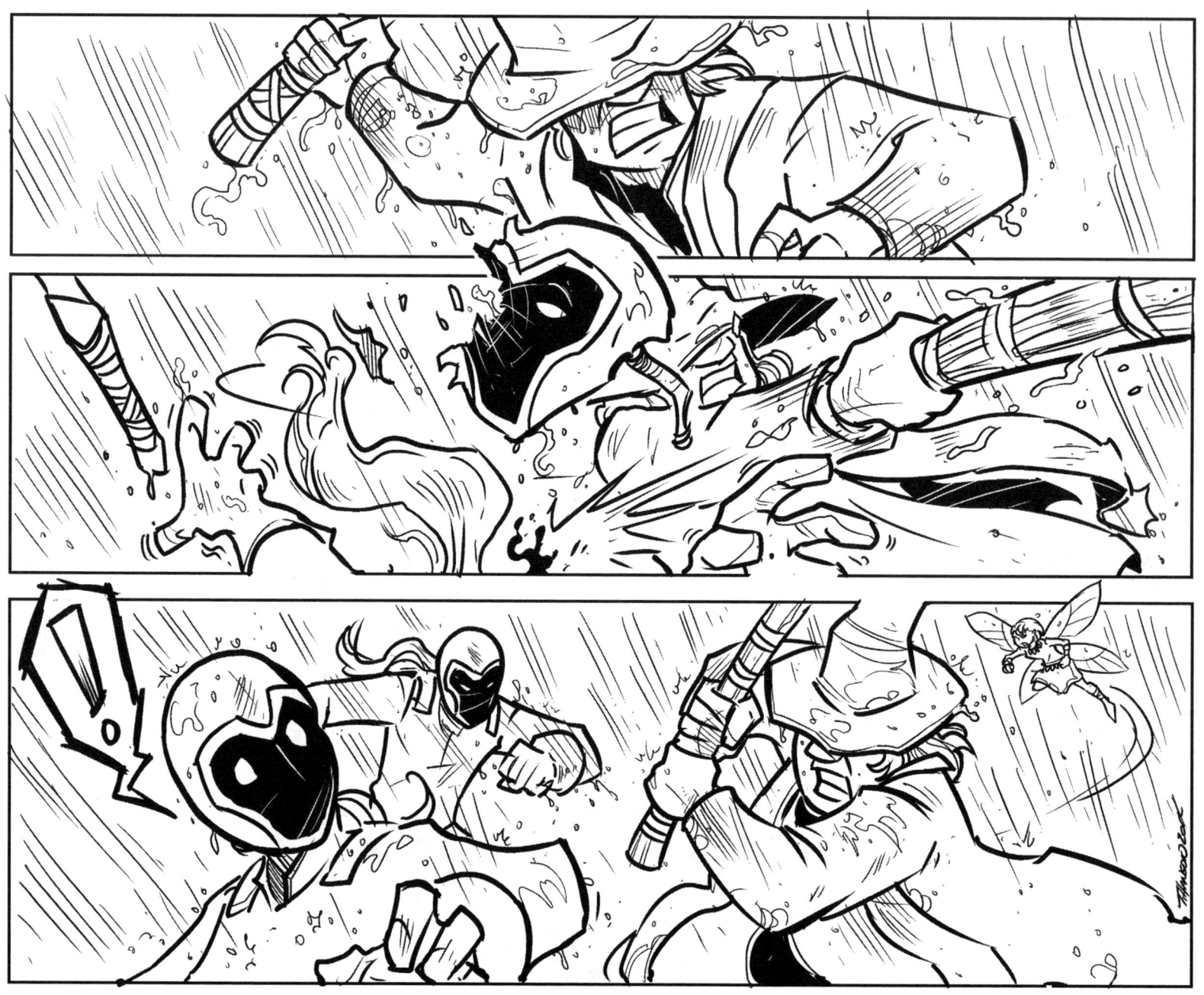

THUNK

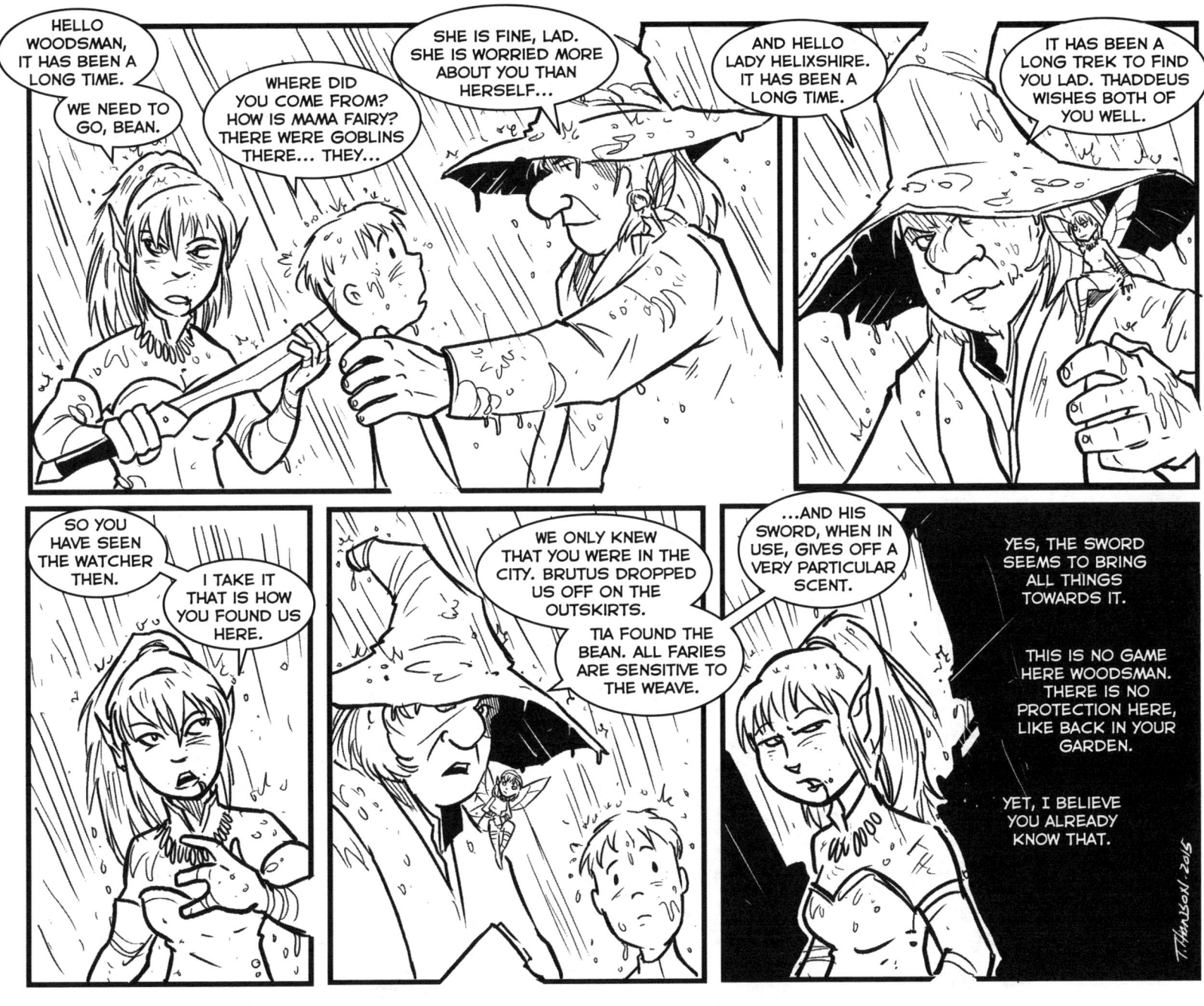

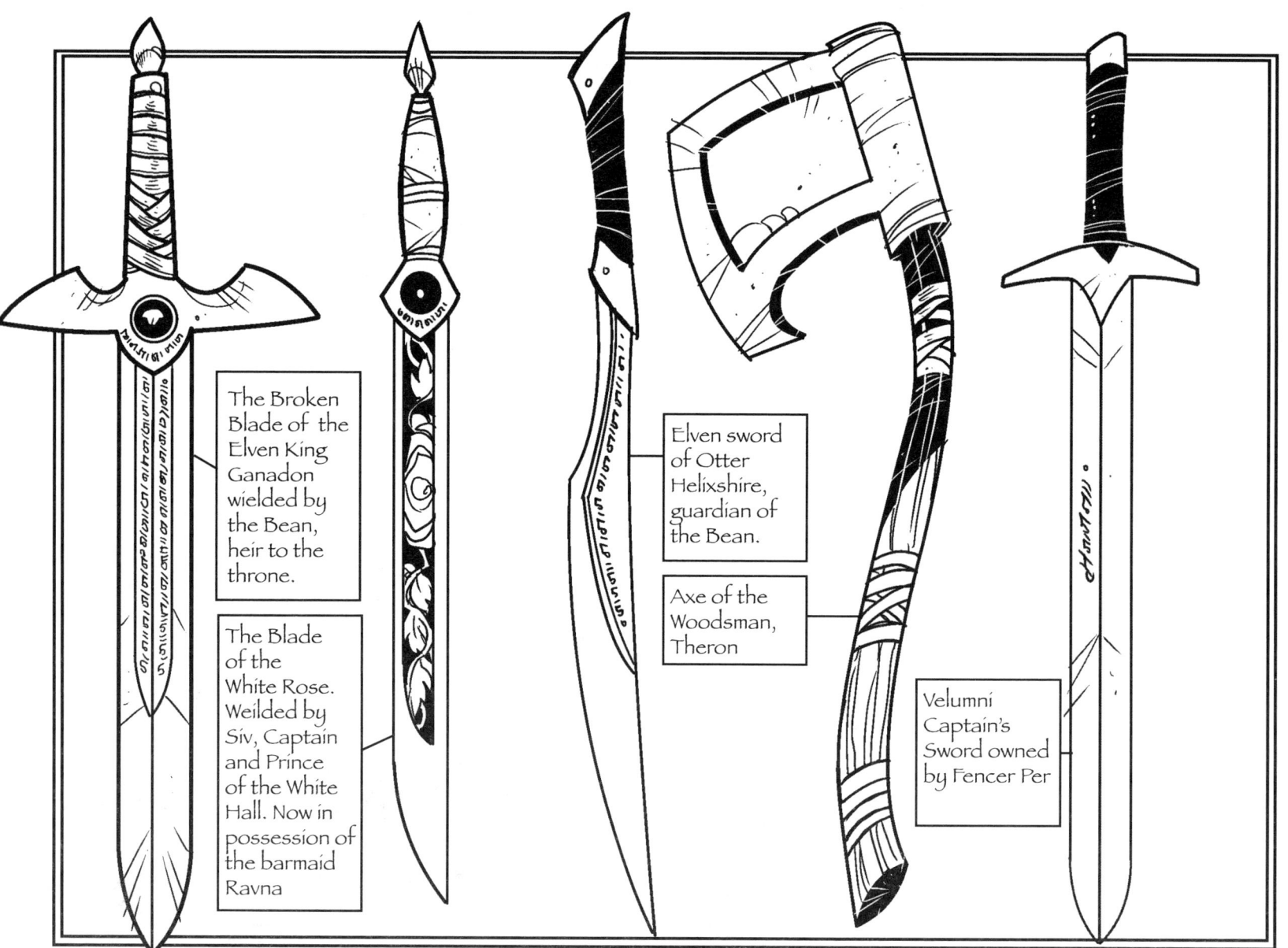

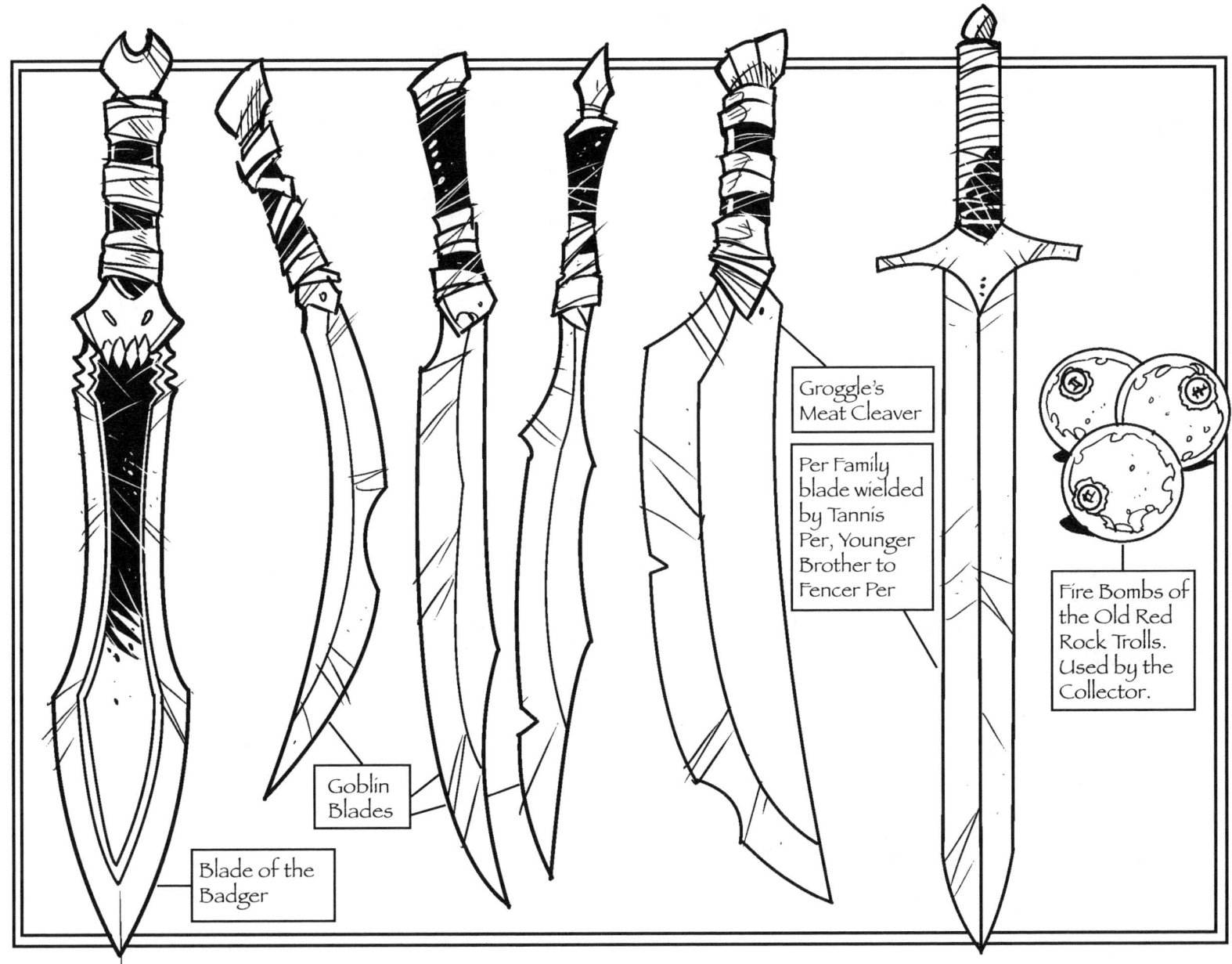

Thank you to the following people who made this dream possible. I could not have done this without your support.

Rebecca and James Hicks
Kevin Coulston
Nolan Tolman & Family
Ross Demma
Mike Scigliano
Adam Hansen
J. Patrick Walker
Marc D. Long
David Workman
Noah Wexo
Ken Malidore
William Weist
Aaron Edwards

KLH
Matthew McCallum
David George
Ivan Yagolnikov
Jeremy Rowland
Anne Thornton
Christopher Mangum
Kristopher Volter
Lic. Jorge Carlos II Cavazos
Galas
Benjamin Strom
Dragon Squad
Durgs
Heidi Berthiaume
Nate Hendon
Gary Kacmarcik

Paul C. Cook
Eileen Walsh
Jennifer Ryan
Dan Sudkamp
Mouin Quiroz
Mel Dumenko
William, Celesta, and James McKinley
Nick Malave
Carlos
Richard Higginson
Chad Andrew Bale
Katherine & Elizabeth Rowe
Andreas Walters
Anders Holgersen
Calissa Moore
Terry Cook
Alex "Monsterchef" Neilson
Andrea Austin
Jonathan Hager
Andrew Tribe
Scott Green
Cassandra Hanson Lloyd
Brad Dancer
Andrew R Hopkins
Xavier Sala
Shawn Harnden
Gerolf Nikolay
Kristin Marie Lear
DamoWela
Brett Abbott

J Doe
J. Cebron Cook
Timothy Mason
Margaret M. St. John
Josh Maher
Rod Hynes
David C. Bahrt
Christopher D. Sandford
Yin Yin Leong
Syndi Keats
Gigi Boudville
Susan Atar
Alice Bentley
Amy Ratcliffe
Kimberly Howe
John MacLeod
Mark DiBlasi
Jill
Kristin
Phil Batey
Jesper ørskov Søndergaard
Steve F. Lefebvre
One Skunk Todd
Shelley Eutizi
Mathieu Doublet
Mike Spring
J.Rencher
Patrick Scullin
Jason Schlueter
Victoria D. Morris
Steve Hansen

Patrick Coyle
Craig Lee
Collin
Cheryl DF09
Jennifer
Jason Brower
TuxedoGin
Jens Bejer Pedersen
Michael David Johas
Mike Kunkel
The Viola's
Brian Sikkenga
Stein Gunnar Bakkeby
Marc Angstadt
karley
Betsy Abbott
Clint D. Johnson
lerolabell
Franck Martin
Jason Oren
Pamela Park
Matthew Shultz
Deborah Jordan
John Peacock
Michael & Michelle Johnson
Steven Moy
James Brewer
David "DJ" Carsten
Phil Layman
Layla & Hannah Kirschner
Valentina "Tinasaurus Rex" Catalano
Loren A. Roberts

Scantrontb
Donald Edwards
Curtis Bates
Jessica "DarkWaterSong"
Hawthorne
Brian Miller
Patrick Robbe
Bartoli Francesco
David Vergara
Martin Ewin
Odile Coindreau Neuberg
Tim De Pree
Christopher W Broden
The Butler Family
Amos Joseph
Michael Carson
Scott Murkin
Igmund
Phipps Family
Chaddaï
Gina Curtice
Jenna Tomlin
Jouni Miettunen
JD Calderon
Katherine Crispin
KatieD
Greta & Gavin Zimmerman
Midnight Campaign
Finn and Kirra Duff
Don Koch
The Kemp Family - Melvin, Jennifer and Benton
William Lohman

Danny Cordell
Fluffboll
Joey Civin
Ruthie M.
Charles Ettinger
Bradley Paul Williams
Matt Bittner
To the King Men
Mikey Brooks
Craig
Gerald Campbell
Slade Eide-Ettaro
Steve Tracy
Dustin Roberts

John Roberts
Blair
Liam Simmons
Larry Tyner
Monica Lang
Victor Briseno
Marc-André Laurence
Erin Hewett
Olivier Lefevre
Saxony Betts
Jala Prendes (Neon Skies Studio LLC)
Shannon Woods
Lawrence Gill

Brett
Trenton Wynter
Dan
Geoff Bowers
Vince Bayless
SHL
Frank Tipler
Ondrea Graye
Chris, Isaiah, & Jimmy Call
johnnyhath
Stewart Kramp
Nathan Rackley
Joby Scott Nothnagel
Vonda M. Sargent
Kevin Pointer
Ksenia Winnicki

Robert Hynes
Coral Mitchell
Jacob W Hull
Will & Liz Morris-Julien
John Idlor
Wade C Harrison III
Harald Demler
Michael and Isaac Rutter
Gregory Sparks
Sean & Karis Chvatal
The Niles Family
Owen John Ryan
Michael Gebhard
Quek Jia Jin
John Rouff
Keri A

Bruce Cawdron
Rich Clabaugh
Joris
Kelly
Ben "Neb!" Girven
Gilbert A. Heredia
Steven K. Watkins
Vexith Gaming
Scott Early
Andy Goldman
Nicholas Vandenberg
EY
Randy O. Knight
Thomas Wener
Cameron Olsen
James Ward
Natasha
Sam Wallace
June Hanson
Robert Lilley
Sven Wiese
Neil B
David Lawrence Sals
Allentine Tanujaya
Darrin Proffitt
Samuel Wolfs
Punmaster & Caleedra Laney
Jason Ford
Kaldran
The Geeky Martinez Family
jdferries
Kenny Wong
Trevor Coward

David Halvorson
Andrew Drew' Weiss
Bradley Hanson
Griggling Games, Inc.
Chris
Jason Howson
John Strobel
Ruth Angelo
Paul M Herkes
Terri Connor
Willow Burr
Scott Mitchell
T. A. Kinde
Michael Earl Hanson
Tony Gullotti
Jay Lofstead
Malia
Thomas Burkard
Little_me
Alexander Yu
Dave & Xephyr Inkpen
Jake Dodd
dreamhappy
Andrea Ristau & Buzz Crisswell.
Joshua Beale
Kiva Duckworth-Moulton
Kathryn & Alexander Woods
Eowyn & Ronan Swift
Justin Boyce
Libbi Rich
Nick Perkins
Zebak LongFang

Toby M. Schreier
Scott and Val Brazier
Brandy Kuschel
Adam J. Monetta
Lee Keegan
Michael Slone
Douglas Russell
Mark 'Grammaw' Becker
Chris Wilson
Aylea Allen
Erin Paxton
Lisa Jones
Edward W Sizemore
Alec Mika
Gary Crowl
Gabe & Eli McBride
Derek "Hendercrazy"
Henderson
CrisisSDK
Casey & Zea Bonanno
Steve Lord
Tim Fleming
Michael Hoffmann
Andrew Vine
Scott & Terry Hanson
Doug Sturtevant
Russell Woll
Steve Espinas
Andy Owings
Martin Rueckheim
John M. Trivilino
Dwayne Plain
Proudpa

Charles III
Otmar, Dawn, Torin, & Elyra
Ben Klazinga
George_GH
Richard Andelfinger
Kevin Albrecht
Anthony Dalo
Sean Murphy
Wyatt Truax
Heather Halliday
William K Walker
Maximus & Edison Jacobs
Ed Kowalczewski
Sheila Lund
Jake Dodd
Bryun Lemon
Clayton Odel Culwell
Brian Y Ashmore
Jericho Cline
Chuck Nelson
Cory Alexander
Jay Lefler
D.J., Karen, Trae & Evan Cole
Aimski
Johnny Splendor
Ira White
XeNaDiCtA
Andrew E.C. Head
Jeremy Shepherd
Don, Beth & Meghan Ferris
Robert "Frank" Ellett
Abby Hanson
Nicholle James

David A. Watanabe
Herman Choi
Charlie Poulin
Lain Mainprize
Bud
Heather Hanson Felker
Thomas Strich
Rob MacAndrew
Ben McCandless
Michael Howard
Julie Dillon
Lloyd Ash Pyne
Allyson Storey
Tira Bunn
Domen Stojić
Elizabeth Betts
Isaac 'Will It Work' Dansicker
Ray Powell
James Cortez Mangles
Sarah Morris
Janice Storey
Lisandro Gutierrez
Christopher Daley
Ashley Baltazar
Paul Doyle

Travis Hanson-
Is an Eisner nominated illustrator with a huge imagination. Travis spends his time in Southern California, with his lovely wife Janell, five children, two cats and a bearded dragon.